The Christmas Night

Michael Machung

Copyright of 2023 Michael Machung of
Touye Moun Horror Publishing LLC.

All rights reserved. This book, or parts thereof, including but not limited to text, images, and fictional characters, may not be reproduced in any form, stored in any retrieval system, or transmitted in any form by any means—electronic, mechanical, photocopy, recording, or otherwise—without prior written permission of the publisher, except as provided by United States of America copyright law. The reproduction, storage, or transmission of any images or fictional characters contained in this book is strictly prohibited without the express written consent of the publisher. Any unauthorized use of these materials may be subject to legal action.

Touye Moun Horror Publishing books may be bought for educational, business, or sales promotional use.

ISBN (Paperback): 979-8-9877087-2-9

ISBN (Ebook): 979-8-9877087-3-6

Acknowledgment

I would like to give my thanks to New York Times Best Selling Editor, David Cashion, and to The Editorial Department's David Argabright for their expertise.

Contents

Chapter 1: Fearless Souls 2

Chapter 2: Acts of Compassion 5

Chapter 3: Another Realm 10

Chapter 4: Miseries 13

Chapter 5: The Woman in White 17

Chapter 6: The Jaws of Death 20

Chapter 7: Heaven and Hell 24

Chapter 8: Someone's Watching 28

Chapter 9: The Dead Rose 31

Chapter 10: Stranger in the Night 35

Chapter 1: Fearless Souls

Wednesday, December 18

"We're reporting live from WRXY News at the Boston Harbor. As you can see, the blizzard, as many are calling 'The Storm of the Century,' is strengthening by the minute. Power outages are occurring across New England. People have been told to stay off the roads as fatalities are piling up. Airports are closed, and the National Guard were called in for emergencies. President Ronald Reagan will be speaking…"

Nolan switched off the battery-powered radio. He then limped up to the second floor, the wooden stairs creaking with each step he took. He held a flashlight tighter than his arthritic hands could really bear, and its beam skimmed over old paintings, antique furniture, and a statue of Hecate, but no light glowed from the torch she held. Without warning, a black cat jumped in his path—he shuddered.

"Dammit, Felix!" He dropped his flashlight. "You scared the hell out of me!" The animal stared with its one eye as the other one was clawed out in a catfight years ago. It stood there expecting something from him. Maybe it wanted to be petted or given a toy to play with. Nolan frowned as he yelled, "Go on, git! You had enough to eat!" The cat then scurried away into a dark corner of the house, camouflaging itself.

Nolan then entered Sonia's room—a situation that had not scared him since the Great Depression, when, as a child, the onus was on him to provide for his family when his parents were unemployed and destitute. It wasn't easy living in that house infested with rats and roaches, but he made it through and was hailed as the family's savior. The words he always held dear to his heart were those intoned by Franklin Roosevelt, "The only thing we have to fear is fear itself." With that encouragement, he trudged on like an armored spirit heading to war.

"That damn storm ain't letting up," Nolan muttered, closing the door behind him. "There's no more medicine," he whispered to his wife. "How's Sonia? Is she… getting better?"

"Our granddaughter… our beautiful granddaughter… is the same. Still sick and no appetite," Laura said somberly while gripping Sonia's hand.

She looked over at Sonia and saw an angel fighting for her life, fighting to be with her grandparents, the ones most important to her. Above Sonia's head was a crucifix of Christ staring down at her, shedding tears and bleeding for the world's sins.

"Grandma," Sonia uttered, "Saw a shadow in my room last night… scary man."

"No need to worry, Sonia, it wasn't real. It's stress. Just stress."

Nolan's eyebrows lowered and pulled closer together. "I tried getting through to Nurse Gillian… lightning must've hit the phone line outside; no connection," he said while rubbing his wife's shoulders. "We'll get through this… Sonia will snap out of it… we'll be celebrating Christmas… together… like we always did!"

Across from where he stood was a statue of Santa Claus on the nightstand, holding a bag of gifts.

"Oh, darling. I hope you're right," she said with fear in her voice. The two embraced.

Chapter 2: Acts of Compassion

At Westview Hospital, outpatients, as well as medical workers, were stranded. Complaints echoed through the corridors as they waited for the storm to pass so they could go home and see their loved ones if they were still alive. Their nerves were worn thinner by the minute as they were left with little choice— it was either wait out the storm or head out and freeze to death.

Far down one hall was Gillian Keller, a young blonde nurse who always placed patients before herself. Over the years, her compassionate nature made some believe she was Florence Nightingale incarnate, while others thought of her like a family member they never had. Some even joked that she was a nurse from *The Twilight Zone.* No one will ever forget, though, when she cared for Trinity, a dying prostitute—AIDS was her death sentence, and she was given five months, but under Gillian's care, she lived another five years. No one knows how she did it; Gillian's mystique would confound doctors for centuries to come.

"Doctor Langston, Sonia's my best friend, and I can't get through to her grandparents," Gillian said disquietedly into the phone. "I'm going to have to drive to her estate to treat her… she could be dying!"

"That'd be suicide!" the doctor thundered. "Power lines are

down, roads are blocked, a curfew is in place, two-hundred fifty-seven people have died—You'd be risking your life; there's no way you can reach her! I know how much Sonia means to you. Believe me, she really matters to me too, but there's only so much you can do to help someone. With her weak immunity, the influenza infection could kill her any moment. Do you understand?" the doctor asked.

"Look. I'm in this to save lives, and I have to try." Gillian cupped her hand over the receiver so no one could eavesdrop on their conversation. "That's the oath I took, and if that girl dies, I'll feel responsible. And not to mention… it's Christmas."

The doctor put down the phone beside a bottle of Jack Daniel's, but he shoved the whiskey away, the temptation failing this time. He then drew a deep breath and rubbed his face, "There's a lot of your father in you. He never cared for his own life as much as he did those of his patients. People like you two are in short supply, I must say." He glanced over at a picture of himself with Dr. Keller, posing in front of Westview Hospital—those were the days. "Okay. Do what you think is right. If you really believe you can get to that mansion safely, then go ahead—do it."

Gillian beamed. "Oh, thanks so much, Doc! Thank you for understanding!"

"Yeah, yeah, yeah. We've been through these situations before, and we came through. I'm fortunate to have a nurse as resilient as you, Gillian. We can't lose you because lives depend on it," he said emphatically but still worried that she wouldn't make it.

"Oh my God, thanks again. I'll be all right! I promise, and I always keep my promises, you know that." The call ended.

Okay, great. I didn't think he was going to let me do it. Good thing I planned this trip carefully... or I would die! Gillian clocked out for the day but couldn't go home. She peered through the window and saw nothing but white as the storm raged on. All of a sudden, someone from behind grabbed her shoulder, startling her.

"Gillian."

The nurse spun around.

"Oh, I'm sorry. I didn't mean to scare you."

"That's okay. Just make yourself known next time, Yolanda," Gillian said, mildly irritated. "So, what's up?"

"I just listened to Peter Jennings on the radio... the storm's not letting up."

Gillian placed her hand on her head and drew a deep breath. "I know, it's getting worse. Boston's completely covered. But I have to leave for a patient's house; it's a life-or-death matter."

"What?!" After calming down, she looked at the nurse sympathetically. "It's that Sonia girl, isn't it?"

"Yes," Gillian said, tight-lipped.

Yolanda sighed. "She lives too far out, like... a hundred-fifty miles out in the countryside. If you haven't noticed, the weather's too severe."

"I know that, but I've been taking care of her for years. We also grew up together; she's like a sister to me. It's a risk I'm willing to take, and nothing's stopping me." Gillian took another deep breath. "It's been a week since I treated her. She needs medical attention, or she'll die. Simple as that," she said with a shrug.

"I love you, but girl, you're crazy," Yolanda replied, shaking her head.

"I know I am. That's why we're friends!" Gillian laughed nervously as they hugged.

"I gotta get back to the office, or Doctor Langston will be on me faster than a speeding ticket. You'll be in my prayers."

Gillian frantically headed to the exit, barely acknowledging her coworkers and even those she'd been working with for years. She even ignored a Santa impersonator while ringing his bell and wishing everyone a Merry Christmas; her only focus was on saving a life.

Chapter 3: Another Realm

Thursday, December 19

The blizzard continued pounding the mansion with relentless fury, but it was resilient enough to fight off its wrath. The house had stood there since the nineteenth century and had had its share of problems and overcome them—its age is a testament to that truth. Snow continued building higher around the estate, creating an icy tomb; the massive gusts had blown down the Christmas lights, as well as the beautiful arborvitae trees that surrounded the manor like a leafy moat in the spring and summer.

The power was still out, and darkness prevailed throughout—the rooms and hallways laden with cobwebs—and the spiders crawling everywhere. But the glimmers of a few candles here and there gave off some light… some hope.

"How's her fever?" Nolan asked, his voice trembling.

"It's 104. She needs medicine. And she needs it now!" Laura slammed her fist on the nightstand, almost knocking over the lamp and the Santa statue.

"I know. I know. I'll try calling Gillian one more time. Maybe… I'll get through. Who knows?" Nolan exited the room, unwilling to submit to fear, as the words 'The only thing we have to fear is fear itself' continued running through his mind. He headed downstairs to the landline phone, hoping for an outside connection finally.

Sonia remained lying on her bed, emotionless, with her hands folded on her stomach like a corpse awaiting burial. She drifted deeper into sleep, finding herself in another realm, in another place with her brown hair blowing in the wind, clouds floating passed her, eagles and angels flying above mountains that stretched to eternity. The fragrances of lilacs, hyacinths, apple blossoms, and daffodils wafted on the cool breeze. Her eyes opened wide when she saw children playing with lions and riding on the backs of elephants, along with people dancing and singing hymns together—it was like Shangri-La. She then saw an ancient man clothed in a raiment behind a lectern holding a key; at his left side, a gate. He smiled. But all of a sudden, sulfur permeated the air, a shadow towered over Sonia, the skies turned gray, and she woke up screaming.

Her door flew open. "Sonia, Sonia! I'm right here. It's okay, dear." Her grandmother hugged her, but she barely returned the affection, her body too frail from the sickness.

"Scary man… in dream," she said in a weak voice.

She closed her eyes and went back to sleep; Laura gently laid her back down on the bed. Nolan, after hearing the commotion, shot into the room.

"What happened?"

"She had a nightmare. Any luck getting through to the hospital?"

He exhaled, "None. But I'm not giving up. We're not going to let this take our daughter! We're Hamiltons, we're strong," he said with clenched fists. He sat down and stared off into the past and uttered one word, "Sophia." The memories arose within him like ghosts rising from their graves, "The mistakes we made in raising her. We were too liberal with her, not conservative enough. She never married. Her drug addiction and her troubled boyfriend were too much for us to bear, then she had Sonia—where is she?!" Nolan shouted.

Laura then placed her hand on his shoulder and said softly, "Sometimes I wonder myself where Sophia's at or if she's still alive, but we did our damnedest to help her before she disappeared, but we made sure Sonia was raised better."

Suddenly, a peal of thunder roared, shaking the mansion on its foundation. Nolan dropped his flashlight again, and they quickly held each other.

Chapter 4: Miseries

In the hospital parking lot, where the winds blew ferociously, Gillian walked briskly to her Ford Bronco and brushed off the heavy snow from the windshield as fast as she could—time was running out. She rushed to the rear of the vehicle and placed her medical kit and other necessities in the trunk. She pulled out chains and fastened them around each tire, hoping the long drive would go more smoothly than she had envisioned. At last, she made it behind the driver's seat and let out a sigh of relief.

Looks like I'm all set. Sonia, here I come! She put her truck in four-wheel drive and moved out slowly from the lot. *God, it looks like the Ice Age out here. I guess they don't call it 'The Storm of the Century' for nothing.*

An hour later, while driving on the icy highway, Gillian couldn't help but notice the stranded vehicles, destroyed road signs and collapsed power lines. But thankfully, none were in her way, at least, not yet. To soothe her stress, she popped in a cassette of Billy Idol, her favorite rock star behind Michael Jackson and Madonna.

"Man, this stuff rocks!" Gillian turned up the volume and bobbed her head to the tune of *White Wedding*, something she had always dreamed of having, but unfortunately, Mr. Right never made it around. Then without warning, a giant tree fell across the turnpike as if shoved down by someone. The impact was so hard it vibrated throughout every inch of her truck. Panic overcame her—she swerved, twisting and turning the steering wheel, trying to maintain control, trying to avoid hitting the massive trunk. A few seconds later, her vehicle came to a standstill; all was calm until she banged her hands on the steering wheel. Then Gillian got out, slammed the door, and looked at the tree.

"This is just great!" Gillian screamed. *After fifty miles, I was going good, so good!*

It reminded her of the time when she was a little girl driving with her father to Casey's Creek, their special getaway place. A traffic accident occurred, causing a holdup, and she thought they'd never make it to the creek. But her dad knew of a back way to reach their destination, and they arrived there unscathed. After a day on the water, they returned home that evening with a bucket full of fish—a symbol of salvation according to her superstitious mother.

This memory gave her hope, and she rushed to the passenger's side and rummaged around in the glove compartment for a few seconds before finding what she was looking for. *All right. This map's old but still current; nothing's changed. To the far right is a path that can get me around this tree and back on the highway.*

Through the cold winds, Gillian squinted and spotted the trail. The more she looked at it, the more visible it became to her. Her scowl then changed to a smile. *Looks like I lucked out!* She jumped back into her Bronco and drove slowly onto the path. Trees grazed up against her truck, and the ride on the beat-up road was bumpy. Then the truck got stuck on an incline. She smashed down on the pedal, but the vehicle still wouldn't budge. She turned off the engine and put her head down. *Maybe Doc and Yolanda were right—I went too far with this.*

Gillian jumped out and placed some wooden boards under the rear tires for traction. *This should work since the front tires are chained anyways.* She got back in the vehicle and stepped on the gas, and the Bronco moved out of the muddy ditch, wet dirt spraying everywhere. *Yes! It worked.* Halfway around, she barely saw the open highway, but it was there, welcoming her.

"All right!" She yelled and pumped her fists in celebration. As she was driving through the snowy winds, she looked back on the last twenty-four hours when she woke up in her apartment. She rose from her bed with little sunlight gleaming through the window shades; the winds were picking up. She entered the bathroom and looked into the mirror, and saw a young woman with bags under her eyes, chapped lips, and premature wrinkles. But she ignored what she saw; life went on. Gillian then peered through her shades and saw her neighbor staring back at her through binoculars. She gave him the middle finger and closed the blinds. Those memories brought a smile to her face but also caused her to miss her ordinary life.

Chapter 5: The Woman in White

"You look tired and hungry, Nolan," Laura said, gently stroking his hair, "Let's go downstairs. I'll make some ramen for us and Sonia; we'll use the coal stove in the basement." She leaned close to her granddaughter. "We'll be back up here in a bit, sweetie." Laura kissed the girl's head.

Sonia heard every word but dozed off into another deep sleep. She found herself back in the same dream, but this time, a woman in white appeared, acting hospitable, kind. "It's okay, child, come with me, come with me," she said as an aura around her glowed. Sonia floated toward her outstretched arms, but suddenly, smoke arose from the depths, and the dark entity returned.

"No! She belongs with us!" it screamed with a monstrous voice.

"NEVER! BEGONE, DEMON!" The lady in white cried out.

Sonia woke up but wasn't screaming; the nightmares were something she was becoming accustomed to. Her grandmother walked in with a bowl of ramen noodle soup with her grandfather behind her.

"You're awake, thank God! Here, drink slowly," Laura said softly.

"I dreamt of a beautiful lady—she was in white. Then… that thing appeared again… the scary man," Sonia whispered.

"SHHHHHH, don't think about those dreams; they don't mean anything." Laura caressed Sonia's hair. "Just stay strong… for us." Laura smiled.

"The… the… storm. Has it gone away?" Sonia asked.

"It'll go away eventually. Don't worry about it. You're safe," Nolan said calmly.

"Is—Gillian—here?" she asked with her eyes barely open.

"No, honey, she's not here yet. We're trying to reach her." Laura looked at Nolan and back to Sonia. "We're trying to reach her."

"Ahhhh, good," Sonia said, starting to smile. In her twilight state, Sonia remembered back in high school when the upper-middle-class girls bullied her:

What's the matter, Sonia? Too poor to attend the prom?

Hey, Sonia! Are you still wearing your mother's old clothes?

Sonia… Are you still living in that creepy house?

You're killing me, Sonia! Can't you afford to wear makeup?

The antagonism seemed unending; she suffered. It got even

worse when their boyfriends flirted with her, making the other girls feel jealous, so much so that they attacked her in the hallway. Along came Gillian, who stuck up for her. They became friends, and a special bond formed. Sonia's eyes closed and drifted off.

Chapter 6: The Jaws of Death

Friday, December 20

A few hours had passed, and Gillian found herself 90 miles from the Hamiltons' estate. *Driving 30 miles per hour isn't my thing, but I'm making good headway. I hope to get there tomorrow sometime; the snow's picking up, and the storm's gaining strength—I can feel it pushing up against my car. And I'm getting hungry… really hungry.*

There was a sudden violent jolt, but Gillian safely guided the vehicle to the side of the highway as far as possible.

"Dammit! What now?!" Gillian slammed her hands on the dashboard, causing it to crack a little. "A damn blowout!" she yelled. *I must've driven over something sharp on that path I took to get around that damn tree.*

Exhausted, she got out and found a flat tire. She went around to the back of the vehicle and pulled out a spare, a lug wrench, a jack and threw them to the ground with force. As she was changing the tire, the cold wind momentarily froze her body. She regained her strength and resumed the work. *Almost finished.*

Out of her peripheral vision, she saw a dark shadow quickly approach her. It then became a solid entity, rubbing against her body and licking her face. *Oh my God… it's a bear. What do I do? I'll just stay still, and maybe it'll go away.*

The bear then walked around her truck, sniffing at the windows. *Shouldn't it be hibernating?*

It stood over six feet tall and began pushing the Bronco. It then got back down on all fours, looked around, and roared. Gillian froze even more, thinking she might become its next meal.

Then the bear lost interest in the vehicle, and, fortunately, Gillian, as well—and wandered across the icy highway, disappearing into the woods. At last, she finished her last step in getting the spare placed on and fastening an extra chain around it.

Yes! It's done. Now I've got to get out of here in case that thing comes back!

After eating her meal, she continued on her route for another ten miles to get away from the area where the bear was lurking, pulled over, read a little bit of a science fiction novel called *The Empyrean,* and went to sleep for the rest of the night, as the moon shined on her vehicle.

Chapter 7: Heaven and Hell

Saturday, December 21

Felix, the cat, entered Sonia's room and hopped on the chair where Laura had been sitting. It usually jumped on Sonia's lap for attention, but not this time. Its one eye stared at her as she lay sleeping under her covers. Its senses detected there was something wrong with her. It meowed and sat watching over her like a guardian angel.

Deep in her dream, Sonia found herself back in paradise with the woman in white. She toured her around the heavenly realm, enlightening Sonia of its purpose and those who rule it.

"I love this place… I don't want to leave," Sonia cried with a smile.

"Everyone loves it here, which is why they never want to leave. Look how happy everyone is." The woman in white gestured around her with an open hand.

In an instant, food and drink appeared in the woman in white's hands. "Here, have some ambrosia and nectar. It's good for you," she said with a smile.

"Ah, thank you!" Sonia consumed the victuals without hesitation. "This stuff is really good!"

Sonia noticed something. "Those two kids playing together near the stream, I know them! That's Maria and her brother, Ethan. They went missing two years ago. They were never found."

"Yes. I'm afraid they were kidnapped and murdered. But they're at peace now. Everything's fine." The woman in white smiled.

As they continued walking together, Sonia stopped, "Oh, I know him over there too," she said, pointing. "That's Henry Hansley. He took his own life last Christmas after his wife left him—I'll never forget that."

Out of the clear blue, a golden retriever jumped on Sonia, causing them both to fall to the ground.

"Oh, Buddy! I missed you so much!" Sonia tickled her dog while the woman in white looked on laughing.

Buddy was licking her face as she tickled him like she used to do when he was alive. The day when a drunk driver struck Buddy dead had left an indelible imprint on her.

After the happiness settled down, Buddy ran away, the smell of sulfur returned, and a clawed hand grabbed Sonia's shoulder. She spun around and woke up screaming.

Felix flew off the chair, and Laura rushed into the room,

asking, "Oh, sweetie, are you okay?" She sat on the bed and scooted closer to Sonia.

"I... think so," Sonia replied.

"It's those nightmares again, huh?" Laura asked.

Sonia nodded.

"You're drooling." Laura wiped the spittle from her face. "Try to stay awake... we'll be here."

Laura heard the sounds of footsteps rushing up the stairs. It was Nolan. He tripped because of his bum leg, but he got up unfazed, nothing stopping him. She quickly got up and met Nolan, who was out of breath, in the doorway.

"I checked the phone... we have reception!" Nolan rejoiced.

"So let's call the hospital. I hope Gillian isn't stranded there... time's running out," Laura said quietly to her husband before running downstairs to the phone and dialing Westview Hospital.

"Westview Hospital. Yolanda speaking. How can I help?"

"Yolanda, it's Mrs. Hamilton, whose daughter is very sick with the flu. Is Nurse Gillian there?" she asked in a panicked tone.

"Ah, yes. She left yesterday to get to your house!"

"Thank God! She hasn't made it back yet; I hope she's okay."

"I'm not sure what's going on. We haven't heard from her, but the lines have been down," Yolanda replied.

"Yes… I understand. We'll be watching out for her! Thank you so much, sweetie… and Merry Christmas!" Laura said in a bitter tone.

"Merry Christmas to you, too."

Laura put down the receiver.

"She's… on her way here?!" Nolan's brow furrowed. "That's great, but I hope she's okay out there!" he said with concern.

"I know. I know. I pray to God nothing's happened to her," Laura said. "She's such a special person. One like her comes around every hundred years or so."

Sonia began coughing uncontrollably.

Chapter 8: Someone's Watching

Sunday, December 22

The snow was picking up again. Gillian, still shaken up from her bear encounter, quickly switched on her defroster and windshield wipers at maximum speed. To her delight, she spotted a Circle K gasoline station through the storm in the distance. *Ah, great. I need more fuel… I'm getting low!*

After making it to the station, she got out and began fueling up the Bronco. Her teeth chattered, her hands shivered, and her mind raced. All she wanted was for all this to come to a gracious end: the blizzard and Sonia's sickness. At Christmas, she never asked for anything and, in general, preferred the role of giver and not receiver; it gave her a feeling that was incomparable to any other.

Suddenly, a pickup truck that looked as if it was in dire need of an overhaul pulled into the station and parked next to the convenience store, but no one got out of it. Gillian noticed and thought it was odd as to why it would stop beside the store when there was no one inside—all the doors were locked, and all the other pumps were available for use.

Gillian tried ignoring the truck, but her nerves fueled her paranoia, and she sensed someone was watching her through the dark, dusty windshield. All she could make out, though, inside the truck were funny toy feet dangling from its rearview mirror. *Maybe the guy's lost and looking at a map, but something's telling me that's not the case.* She kept her eyes steady on the fuel meter—*C'mon, c'mon! Hurry up! I want out of here!* Her fear was eating away at her.

Finally, the tank was topped up, and the pay machine read $25.24. Gillian rushed inside the Bronco to grab her checkbook. As she wrote one out, her fingers were shaking, and the numbers and characters looked like insane scribbles. She pulled out another check and started over again. This time everything was written legibly. She immediately ran to the store's front and slid it under the door, ignoring the truck whose engine was still running.

Now to get out of here for good! She thought to herself with a sigh of relief.

As she drove up to the stop sign, the pickup also pulled out. *That bastard's following me! That's okay… I have my gun under the seat. Hopefully, it won't get violent, and he'll just go away; twenty-five more miles and I'll be at Sonia's.*

Gillian put her right blinker on and pulled out slowly onto the icy road, driving toward her destination. The truck also made a right turn but didn't use a blinker. Her quivering hands clutched the steering wheel and kept to her thirty-mile-per-hour speed; going any faster could be deadly, she realized. The truck then began blowing its horn. *What does he want?* She gazed in her mirror and saw the battered truck tailgating her. Her heart skipped a beat, but it kept pumping furiously.

Then the truck started bumping her rear; she lunged forward, almost banging her head up against the windshield. "YOU SON OF A BITCH!" Gillian screamed. She then pulled over to the shoulder of the road, grabbed her gun, and got out. The truck also pulled over onto the roadside and stopped, but no one stepped out. Without hesitation, though, she shot a few warning shots in the pickup's direction. It then peeled off, disappearing into the snowy wind.

That did it! He got the hint not to fuck with me! I'm more than willing to finish it if he comes back, Gillian thought to herself.

Chapter 9: The Dead Rose

Monday, December 23

Waiting and hoping for Gillian to arrive, Laura and Nolan were comforting Sonia the best they could. Her fever had increased, her pulse had gotten slower, and her body even seemed thinner; things were looking bleak. The mansion's wooden frame creaked from the weight of the snow, sounding like it could give at any moment. Downstairs, the blizzard's winds burst through one of the windows, showering glass everywhere. Terrified, Laura clung to her husband.

"Nolan," she whispered. "I think I hear something... it's Gillian. I know it's her!" The Hamiltons rushed downstairs to greet her.

At that moment, Sonia was dreaming. The woman in white opened her arms, and Sonia latched onto her; the bearded man with the key then opened the gate; the scary man who was trailing her roared and fell into a dark abyss; he was no more. This time, Sonia didn't wake up.

The Hamiltons rushed downstairs to greet Gillian. As Nolan and Laura opened the door, Gillian approached them, covered in snow and carrying a medical kit; her face was white, her hair disheveled, and the Bronco behind her appeared mangled like it had been attacked by wild animals. Laura could only imagine the trials and tribulations the girl had experienced to get there and quickly embraced her.

"Thank God you made it. We were worried to death! She's upstairs in bed."

"Everything will be okay, Mrs. Hamilton!" Gillian assured her.

Gillian rushed upstairs into Sonia's bedroom and saw her friend lying on the bed, not moving a muscle, her skin looking very pale. She checked her heartbeat with the stethoscope—nothing. She performed CPR… still nothing. Gillian's emotions took over, and she burst into tears, knocking her medical kit to the floor. Felix ran out of the room as the Hamiltons hurried in.

"Sonia's gone. I… tried making it here as fast as possible. I'm so sorry!" Gillian said with her eyes full of tears while holding Sonia's body. Laura sobbed as Nolan looked down and muttered a few prayers, ending them with the sign of the cross. Gillian then pulled up the sheet to fully cover Sonia's body.

"Nolan," Laura whispered. "I remember Sonia mentioning a woman in white." Suddenly, it dawned on her who that was, and the hair rose on her arms. "Oh, my God."

"Yes. I remember," Nolan said. "It was the death angel."

The winds then grew stronger, blowing off more shingles and stripping away more wood from the house as if the storm was mourning in its own destructive way. Laura knew it would be twice as dangerous for Gillian to return to Westview than it was when she left her town. The thought of losing another life within the same night would be too much for the elderly lady to bear.

"Gillian, you're going to stay here for the night. I have a guest room. Make yourself feel at home." Laura forced a smile.

After she wiped away her tears, Gillian's face shone with relief as she, too, knew her life would be on the edge had she left. "Thanks so much, Mrs. Hamilton. I'll… get showered up and try to get some sleep." They both hugged each other tightly.

Chapter 10: Stranger in the Night

Tuesday, December 24

It was almost midnight, there were no gifts under the bare Christmas tree, and the stockings that hung from the chimney were empty. As the sun fell, the blizzard restrengthened—the night wasn't looking good. Nolan was sound asleep, but Laura was wide awake, thinking about the good times with Sonia. Thoughts of her looking over them seeped into her fragile mind. She truly missed what a masterpiece her granddaughter truly was during her life: her poetry, her love for animals, her giving to charity, her voice—her smile. Laura tried getting sleep but to no avail. She slowly arose from the bed, lit a candle, and walked downstairs, thinking only of Sonia.

As she made it down the steps, silhouettes of reindeer crossed the window shades, but Laura didn't notice them. The grandfather clock struck twelve midnight, and the bells chimed for a few seconds but stopped. Then, suddenly, there was a knock at the door.

Who can that possibly be? Laura thought to herself.

She put down her candle and opened the door without hesitating, something Nolan warned her not to do, given that they lived in the middle of nowhere. Standing in front of her was a white-bearded postman holding a letter made of what looked like papyrus, which seemed strange. He said nothing, just looked Laura straight in the eye with no expression, no emotion. She grabbed the letter and motioned the postman to come in, and closed the door behind him.

"Who are you? You… can't be the postman." She squinted at him in wonder. "It's too late at night, and the weather's too treacherous for delivery. How did you get here through the blizzard?" Laura asked. Then she took a second look. "And you don't even have any snow on you?"

Again, he said nothing and only looked at the letter in her hand; she got the hint and read it.

"Dear Grandma and Grandpa,

I'm safe in Heaven. I have found happiness and joy where I am. I shall not forget the great memories we had together as a family. I miss you both and look forward to us reuniting again. We are all waiting for you and Gillian to cross over. I love all of you so much.

—Sonia Hamilton"

"OH MY GOD!" Laura cried out, and she fell trembling to the floor, gasping for air. The mysterious postman gently helped her up, and she hugged him tightly. She then pulled away and looked down while she wiped away her tears. As her vision cleared, she looked up to see presents under the tree, over-stuffed stockings hanging from the mantle, and fresh garland draped gaily around the room.

Laura turned around, and the postman was gone... disappeared into thin air. *A spirit?* she wondered. Her astonishment drove her out front to see where he had gone. At first, she noticed that the blizzard had weakened and fell to her knees, looking down, weeping in the flurries.

Gillian, in her second-story bedroom, also struggled to get to sleep. She then had this compulsion to get up and look out the window. As she looked up, there was an amazing sight to behold, a sight that was the antithesis of the horrors she had faced during her travels and the sight of her friend's lifeless body lying in bed. It was Santa Clause on his sleigh, sailing through the pink skies.

Made in the USA
Monee, IL
15 August 2023

40833666R00025